# AnimaLimericks

# AnimaLimericks

## BY RAYMOND DRIVER

HALF MOON BOOKS

Published by Simon & Schuster

New York • London • Toronto • Sydney • Tokyo • Singapore

HALF MOON BOOKS
Rockefeller Center, 1230 Avenue of the Americas
New York, New York 10020
Copyright © 1994 by Raymond Driver
All rights reserved including the right of
reproduction in whole or in part in any form.
HALF MOON BOOKS
is a trademark of Simon & Schuster.
Manufactured in the United States of America

10  9  8  7  6  5  4  3  2  1

*Library of Congress Cataloging-in-Publication Data*
Driver, Raymond. Animalimericks/Raymond Driver.
p.  cm.  Summary: A collection of limericks about such
animals as the slim penguin named Blair, the odd beaver
from Corning, and the long dachshund named Stretch.
1. Animals—Juvenile poetry. 2. Children's poetry, American.
3. Limericks. [1. Limericks. 2. Animals—Poetry.
3. Humorous poetry. 4. American poetry.] I. Title
PS3554.R554A83  1993  811'.54—dc20  93-12811 CIP
ISBN: 0-671-87232-X

In memory of my father, Raymond,
who loved children, animals and humor

Special thanks to Paul and Eva

There was a young rabbit named Josh
Whose feet he neglected to wash
Till the dirt 'tween his toes
Sprouted veggies in rows,
Such as carrots and turnips and squash.

There was a slim penguin named Blair
Who munched on an ice-cream eclair.
When she finished that one,
She ate twelve more for fun
Till she looked like a black-and-white pear.

There was a poor farsighted snake
Whose eyeglasses happened to break.
That nearly blind fella
Wolfed down an umbrella,
Which opened one day by mistake.

There was a poor croc in despair.
His false teeth were painful to wear.
With relief and delight
He would place them each night
In a fish tank he perched on a chair.

There was a long dachshund named Stretch
Whose owner insisted he fetch.
His front sprang like a shot
Though his tail-end did not.
Now he looks like a pretzel, poor wretch.

Good boy!

There was a giraffe with a flair
For forming her neck like a stair.
From a fourth-story floor
She saved twenty or more
From a blaze that entrapped them up there.

There was a young pig from Tijuana
Who married a pretty iguana.
Soon a baby was born
On a lovely spring morn—
An adorable little piguana.

There was a bored horse whose delight
Was to paint herself both black and white.
With several bold swipes
She splashed on some stripes
And a zebra became overnight.

There was a large panda named Chu
Who loved to partake of bamboo.
Tender shoots he'd devour,
Eating hour after hour,
Till his feet he could no longer view.

There was an old bullfrog from Prague
Who sat by the road on a log.
"Please come kiss me," he cried
To a princess he spied;
So she did and turned into a frog.

There was a sick seal named Ms. Rose
Who went to a doctor she knows.
He advised the young seal,
"Eat a well-balanced meal";
So she balanced a stew on her nose.

There was a wise owl named Sir Matt.
As a judge in a courtroom he sat.
He dismissed in a hurry
An all-canine jury
When he learned the accused was a cat.

There was a bright cobra named Paul
Who thought grammar school was a ball.
The reading and writing
He found quite exciting,
But he liked hisssssss...tory best of all.

There was a parched camel named Scott
Who drank lots of tea very hot.
He would lounge on a rug,
Drinking mug after mug,
Till he looked like a giant teapot.

There was a young hummingbird who
Would hum a fine tune as she flew.
When it came to a hum,
She was never humdrum—
All her tunes were humdingers, it's true.

here was a huge rhino named Lorne
Who loved to eat snacks in the morn.
e had one clever quirk—
s he left home for work,
e would stack doughnuts high on his horn.

There was an odd beaver from Corning
Who liked to cook pancakes each morning.
With a flip of his tail
To the ceiling they'd sail,
Then they'd fall to the floor without warning.

There was an anteater named Betty
Who dined at the Café Rossetti.
Folks watched with great awe
Her mouth shaped like a straw
As she sucked up her plate of spaghetti.

There was a tornado that found
Its way to a neighborhood pound.
All the animals there
Were swept up in the air,
Then it rained cats and dogs all around.

There was an old flea known as Gus
Who lived on a collie named Russ.
Although Russ was his home,
The old flea liked to roam;
So he used a greyhound as a bus.

There was a smart skunk known as Sue
Whose teacher said, "Yes, it's quite true.
You must go on to college
To further your knowledge."
Sue listened and went to PU.

There was a cat prone to explore
Who fell from the thirty-third floor.
She dropped straight to the street,
Landing square on her feet;
And she walked away good as before.

There was a swift centipede, Pete,
Who wanted to run in a meet.
But it took several weeks
To lace up all his sneaks,
By then Pete was too late to compete.

There was a young chimp known as Dot
Who hated to go for a shot.
A shot made her nauseous,
So Dot was precautious
And covered her rear with a pot.

There was a young black bear named Lance
Who won a dance contest by chance.
All the judges expressed
That this bear danced the best,
Till they learned he had ants in his pants.

3